NO REGRETS

No Regrets

A novella

by

JULIANA NICEWARNER

Adelaide Books
New York / Lisbon
2021

NO REGRETS

A novella

By Juliana Nicewarner

Published by Adelaide Books, New York / Lisbon
adelaidebooks.org

Editor-in-Chief
Stevan V. Nikolic

For any information, please address Adelaide Books
at info@adelaidebooks.org

or write to:

Adelaide Books
244 Fifth Ave. Suite D27
New York, NY, 10001

ISBN: 978-1-954351-95-0

Printed in the United States of America

To my mom — my first and best teacher, reader, and friend

Acknowledgements

"Thank you to my parents who never told me that I was good at anything that I wasn't and encouraged me in everything that I was. Thank you to my professors who assigned me far too many projects and gave me the opportunity to get creative in desperation. Thank you to my husband who is always there with a smile and a witticism (which he then lets me plagiarize.) Thank you to Beth who puts up with me all the time, is always there with a new show and tequila, and who weird things happen to — you give me great ideas. And thank you most of all to God without whom I have no ideas at all but an endless stream of writer's block."

The old man was dead – that curmudgeon. It was the kind of funeral you would expect for the eccentric great uncle of a well-to-do family: respectable, utterly typical, clean. The coffin was made of oak – of good enough quality to say to the world, "We've got money to spare" but plain enough to say, "Our associations with this man go no further than blood." The newly-deceased's relatives milled about, uncomfortable, a little cold, like they too were stuffed in the formal, practical box. The cubed cheese was rapidly disappearing. People eat when they're uncomfortable. If you have something to hold in your hands, you feel like you have a purpose. There was condensation beading on the glasses, perilously close to slipping. It was quite cold outside. And quite stuffy inside.

No one had a word to say about him. The man had out-lasted almost all of his direct relations – brothers, sisters. No wife. No children. No real friends. So the only people left to attend his funeral were confused third cousins, annoyed great-grand nieces, stuffy third and fourth removeds, etc. They all made chit chat about the weather and danced around their real concern.

"What a depressing day."

"Yes, the clouds haven't lifted once."

"Terrible weather."

"Yes, you know, I've never been to a funeral on a day that wasn't cold and rainy. Absolutely horrible! Takes the shine out of your shoes, puts wrinkles in your dress."

"Oh yes, I had no idea what the devil to do with my hair today. Horrible! I went out and bought myself a pretty hat to cover it."

"It is a lovely hat."

"Thank you."

The behatted woman was one of the thirds or fourths. Even she didn't understand quite how she was related to the deceased. But as most women with hair dyed a few shades too dark, who have stuffed themselves into loudly patterned dresses perhaps a size or two too small, she was determined to make a show. Atop her frizzy bouffant sat a green velvet hat. She thought it made her look wealthy and distinguished paired with her bright orange dress. She'd picked it up because she thought it was the color of money, and that made her feel very clever. The unhatted one, Molly, to whom she was speaking thought it made her look more like a moldy carrot. Molly, was a little more honest looking – her hair color reflected her age regally, and her dress was sensible, a nice navy to compliment her graying hair.

"Verdant even," said Molly.

"Indeed."

"Speaking of green, do you remember, of course I only went into the house once. But do you remember those green velvet curtains hanging in the bedroom?"

There hadn't been any green velvet curtains in the bedroom.

"No, I don't."

"Odd. I think they were right next to that lovely mahogany chest."

There was no mahogany chest.

"Oh?" She was losing interest. The heat of the room was making her cakey foundation drip onto her chest. Both she and her dress knew that if she ate one bite, she'd pop right out of the straining fabric. Her cheeks were growing flushed from the effort of resisting the cheese tray.

"Yes, and on top of that sat that gorgeous tea-set. What was it called? Meyers? Mischner?" Molly was fully aware that it was called Meissen porcelain and was worth about $3,000. The other figurines that were scattered throughout the house were worth several thousand a piece.

"Something like that."

"Do you know who's getting that?"

This sort of conversation was going on throughout the entire hall. Money-grabbing chitter, nothing to do with the dead man they'd supposedly come to pay their respects to.

At the precise moment that the moldy carrot was opening her mouth to ask her own probing questions about the dead man's fortune, the doors opened. Everyone grew quieter, like they were suddenly ashamed of their ulterior motives for coming to "mourn" in the presence of this newcomer.

She was tall, the kind of woman whose form had never been anything less than svelte. She stood straight. A bit of the damp chill blew in with her, giving an almost eerie sense to her appearance. She gave her jacket a good shake and ran a slim hand over her hair as she searched the room. The door shut with a clank behind her. She saw the other set of doors and walked directly through the hall towards the viewing room. All the eyes followed her. She noticed. She stared straight ahead.

She was in her sixties or seventies. Her slim hands were a little calloused and more than usually wrinkled. But she wore her gray hair like a crown – down, Jayne Mansfield-esque. Her almost wrinkleless skin, however, made her look younger than she was without the air of those who are trying to *appear* young. The woman in orange hated her immediately. The stranger pushed open the doors. As soon as they shut, the people who had been standing by, watching her so patiently, flocked to the doors to look through the little vertical windows into the room beyond.

The casket was at the end of the dark room. The mortuary staff were to take the body to the cemetery. None of the guests were going.

She faltered a little when she saw him. He was wrinkled. When she got to the casket, she rested her hands on the side of it. She couldn't stop staring at the corners of his eyes. The wrinkles were even deeper than she'd thought. His mouth was hard-set. It made a line straight across his face like a mail slot. Her lips parted a little, and a slow sad smile came to her. She lifted that slim hand, warm with life, and placed it on his cold ones.

The onlookers squished against the windows gasped.

"I've never seen that woman in my life."

"The gall!" This was a little muffled. It came from the carrot woman whose mouth was now stuffed with cheese.

"Disgusting!"

"How dare she come in here and spoil such a reverent moment," said Molly. The one who'd just been trying to snatch the Meissen.

"What is she pulling?"

The stranger heard none of this. She stood staring into his face for a minute longer before giving his hand a soft squeeze and backing away. The onlookers saw her mouth move. Then she was turning. With the speed of an exploding firework, the people shot away from the windows and began to chatter again, loudly this time, about the weather and the news. She reappeared to twenty pairs of eyes straining as far as they possibly could without moving their heads. She looked around again. Taking stock.

She'd grab some cheese before she left. She walked purposefully up to the table.

"Oh my," said the carrot lady.

"Excuse me?" The mysterious woman turned slowly to her. "'Oh my' what?"

"Oh my, you. How did you know Andy?"

"From a long, long time ago."

"But where did you meet?"

"We grew up in the same neighborhood." She started to walk away.

"Were you friends?"

"Sort of." She sidled past a clump of people.

"Sort of?"

She sighed and stopped sidling. "Yes, we were engaged."

It got very quiet. At this point, every ear in the room perked up. The stranger's eyes squinted a little and darted about from face to shocked face. She flushed and put down her cube of cheese. The orange lady thought she saw her hands shake.

"Forgive me, how rude. I'm Claire." Out stretched the slim hand.

"Camilla." The orange dress strained, creaked, and wrinkled under the pressure of the arm-movement. "Did you know Andy long?"

"Not really, no." Claire's eyes were fixed on her shoes.

Camilla exchanged glances with a distant family member.

"Have you kept in touch?" Camilla was staring at Claire with a new fascination.

"No, not for years."

"How did you find out about the funeral?"

"Newspaper. I really must be going. So sorry to intrude." Claire shifted her purse to a more secure place on her forearm and started toward the door.

It is interesting to note that on that morning, Claire had been thinking of something quite different from funerals and cubed cheese – *Calvin and Hobbes.* In fact, she hadn't been thinking of anything really except Calvin's latest existential crisis, her coffee, and her hot bowl of oatmeal. As was her custom, she'd woken up, made her breakfast, and crawled back in bed with a tray and a newspaper – the small-town paper she'd read as a child (they gave her a subscription at the same price she'd been paying since she was a kid: a dollar a month. Mailed it all the way from Chicago to New York for free). She still opened the paper to the comics section first like a little kid. *Silly at my age,* she would tell herself as she thumbed eagerly to the section.

This particular morning, she finished the comics and moved through the rest of the paper – politics, fashion, books, eulogies. She'd gotten into the habit of reading the eulogies on Sundays. She recognized too many of the names not to. But today, she froze.

Andreas "Andy" Kovac, dead at seventy-two of chronic bronchitis. No known relatives. Funeral to be held April 15.

She folded the paper back together and put it on her tray. She stared straight ahead at the wall in front of her. There was one patch in the paint that had always bothered her. It had been covered with gloss paint while the rest of the wall was done in flat. It could only be seen in the wee hours when the bright yellow of the morning light shone through the window. She'd always thought it had been shaped rather like a hat.

She felt the tears dripping down her cheeks. She kept clutching the floral comforter on her bed tighter between her fingers, clenching and unclenching her hands. But there were no racking sobs as the tears struck the comforter. Only the quiet grief that comes with the confirmation of something you've felt to be true for a long time.

Because the truth was, he'd been dead for a long time. Dead to her. She'd been twenty-two the last time she'd heard his voice. It had been raining; the memory felt like it came out of some corny movie. His voice had cracked.

She'd known he'd never left the area. *This is what I get for sentimentality,* she thought as she stared at the newspaper. She might never have known. Gone on peacefully without this pull in her gut.

April 15.

She jumped out of bed, dribbling coffee on the comforter as she leapt. *Damn,* she thought through as she looked at the stain covering the flowers. Then she was on her knees, reaching as far under the bed as she possibly could. She felt boxes of photos, some stuffed animals from when she was a child. Shoved against the back was an old leather suitcase. She grabbed the handle and yanked.

In an hour, she'd dressed herself in her best. Like she was trying to impress someone. *Too late.* She walked out into the breakfast room.

"I'll be gone today."

"And tonight?" said an agreeable looking man in a professorial vest. Not one hair was out of place. Not one hair was ever out of place.

"Tonight, too."

"Work?"

"Yes, sudden. I'm off!"

He got one distracted kiss on the cheek before his wife was out the door. This was not unusual. She was often whisked away for work. Mr. Claire Ryan, as he was often called, went back to sipping his coffee.

Claire Ryan had, so far, grown up with the sure knowledge that she was the luckiest and most meaningless girl in the world.

Claire Ryan's father still spoke in a heavy accent that matched his thick understanding of the new world. His shock of red hair, passed on to his children, shouted "Mick!" to everyone he met.

"You don't need to work, Claire. I make enough for the family still. Not until I'm dead in me grave do you need to be slavin' away at the mill, ruinin' your pretty white hands!"

She'd first posed the question before she'd even started school. Why couldn't she work at the mill and make a little extra money for the family? That's what all the other families in the area did. But Danny Ryan was determined – his daughter would be educated. His children wouldn't slave away like the other Irish kids on the block. He would make enough to support his family, or he would go down to the docks and throw himself into the sea.

"Claire, you daft thing. Enjoy your childhood. It's a rare thing."

Her face slacked with disappointment. This broke his heart a little. The one thing he wanted in life was to make absolutely sure that his children never had cause to do anything but smile. And he often told Claire this. He looked into her sad eyes, and she watched as he forced his own face into a sad look like an opera mask. Claire laughed. They'd done this routine since before she could speak.

Danny wanted to give the world to his daughter, and to him, the world meant getting her all the way through high school. Maybe even to some kind of certificate. Danny Ryan worked his first shift back in Ireland at eight. He got schooling on Sunday mornings from the Parish priest, but his education didn't go beyond some reading and light figuring. And he'd lost his childhood the first day he came home with a few cents in his pockets. His daughter wouldn't do the same.

The Ryan family had stayed in Ireland through the whole famine. Almost all the other Irish families in that quarter of Chicago had come over in the 1850s because they had to. The Ryans came over in the 1930s because they wanted to.

Like every good Irish Catholic, the Parish and the Pub were equal to Danny. The Parish was the place you went to have communion with God. The Pub was the place you went to have communion with everyone else. He and Claire had strolled into the pub on the corner the first day they'd come to Chicago. He was in the area looking at the very house he sat in now when he'd decided he needed a bit of refreshment. Claire dragged behind him a bit looking a little green. She hadn't quite been herself since the boat passage. Seasickness was mean to young kids, and Claire was only six at the time.

There was a golden bell on the heavy oak door and a great big embellished sign that read "O'Flattery's" in a flourishing gold script over a dark green background. Inside, smoke billowed up from twenty different clay pipes and created a dense, homey fog. Claire looked up at her father through the thick smoke and saw him take a deep breath. She did, too. *Mmm.* It smelled like the pubs back home. She clung to Danny's hand

and looked around in wonder. The rest of the country so far hadn't looked like Ireland. But this place did.

"Lads! A newcomer!" The barkeeper, Mr. O'Flattery himself, had his shirtsleeves rolled up past his elbows, and the pipe waggling in the corner of his mouth made it look like he chewed on his words before they came out. He slid a tall glass of stout down the bar to Danny. "Where abouts are ye from, man?" His accent was faded. It had been passed down through as many generations as the curtains on the windows.

"Ireland." Danny smiled proudly into his beer as the chatter went around the bar.

"A sham," laughed a portly man already several glasses deep.

"Are ye daft?" asked the barkeeper. "His accent is as fresh as the fish coming off the boats this morning."

Danny lifted his glass off the counter towards the barkeep. Claire watched as the Irish twinkle, gone for a few hours there while he was desperately looking for a home, came back in Danny's eyes.

Every day in the Ryan home was the same. They'd wake up with the rest of the neighborhood, a few hours before dawn. Peggy Ryan sliced potatoes in her dressing gown, her hair still in curlers under the patterned silk scarf she brought with her from the old country, cracked a few eggs, and threw it all in a skillet to cook for either far too long or far too short. The little ones tromped into the kitchen with a single blanket huddled over their heads, looking like an eight-legged turtle. By this time in the morning, Claire was already stepping out the door. She watched the young siblings with a twinge of bitterness. *They* were allowed to head straight to the woodstove. *They* were sung to by Mother as she pulled breakfast together. *Claire* had to jump immediately from bed into her galoshes and too-thin cotton coat and tend to the chickens. Gone were her days of sitting by the fire and listening to Mother's sweet voice as she served the runny eggs. Claire's father had decided that becoming Master of Chickens was a good compromise between Claire's desire to work and his desire for her to enjoy her childhood. So there was Claire – taking a deep breath and tromping out into the snow to tend the damn hens.

The Ryan house had what not many others in the neighborhood had – a yard. The Ryan's had no more use for frivolity than anyone else, so the yard became the chicken coop as fast as Danny Ryan could scrape together the money for that first hen. If Claire had tried, she could've hopped out of the back door and landed on the roof of the coop. In fact, she did try on occasion, in the summertime when there were enough degrees in the temperature to allow for such wasted time.

But not today. Today, the Illinois wind made for a brisk 12 degrees Fahrenheit on the battered thermometer stuck to the side of the house. *Not the worst, not the best.* She peeked over the fence quickly into the Kovak's yard. They also had a chicken coop.

"Clairy!" Her mother's shout pulled Claire into the house as the chill nipped at her heels.

After both the chickens and the people of the house had been adequately fed, Peggy dressed, layed out each child's clothes, inspected their freshly scrubbed faces, patted them on the backsides, and trotted them out the door to Mass.

"On with you. If we're late on earth, how do you expect to make it into Heaven before Saint Peter closes his pearly gates? Good habits got to be formed. If you're late to Mass, the Lord doesn't count it." And so on and so forth. Her words were like steel wool for the soul, but her smile could warm the heart in even the bitterest Chicago winter.

The bright spot in Claire's morning came when she saw all the other families shuffling and squawking into the parish – they looked the Ryan's hens and roosters followed by their chicks. Her friend Maggie Kovak lived next door and always left her house about two minutes after the Ryans did. The Kovak's had one more kid than the Ryans. One more kid, two more minutes.

As the Kovaks caught up with the Ryans, the two flocks merged together. Maggie and Claire linked arms, and Claire asked all her burning questions about what it was like to be "normal."

"What time did you go to work yesterday?"

"Oh, five o'clock in the morning, just like Ma." Maggie's little curved nose pointed up in the air, like she thought her job brought her an inch or two closer to God.

"Christ!" Claire looked behind her quickly to see if the grownups had caught her. They seemed to be paying an awful lot of attention to the road at their feet and none at all to the children. "I mean, goodness, that sounds important."

A head with more hair than face on it popped up between them. "I get to go to work next year!" Maggie's kid brother Andy craned his neck and walked on tip-toe so he could put his head in between Maggie's and Claire's. He was only a couple years younger than the big girls, but he might as well have been a cooing infant for all they cared for him. Claire didn't really think he was so bad. He didn't pick his nose like Jonny Fitzgerald or try to swing from Claire's braids like Peter O'Brian. But he was too little to be friends with them.

The parish was a five-minute walk from home. And in the wintertime, it felt like an eternity. Claire would wedge herself into Maggie's coat with her. It was stocky wool, bought with

Maggie's own money and conveniently two sizes too big to last her longer and, of course, to fit both her and Claire inside.

The parish was blacker and more ominous than the parishes back in Ireland. It loomed like a menacing governess over the one-story Protestant church next door. The Kovak/Ryan party would split here at the doorways – the Ryans would shuffle into the somber Parish, stomping the snow off their shoes, and the Kovaks would rush into the church. Claire would dip her fingers in the holy water and watch Maggie's bouncing braids with their bright ribbons disappear into the church. She imagined a whole other world inside. One without a scary German priest who bent down to look you in the eye and tell you to spit out your gum. All the priests in Chicago seemed the same to Claire. They all had scary bushy eyebrows that they waggled for emphasis and their breath smelled like salted pork. She pictured the pastors in the Protestant church being jolly fat Santa Claus types, always ready with a piece of candy while the Fathers were dolling out Hail Marys and finger wags.

Her feet were going numb as she rested on the kneelers. Mother Mary was staring at her so hard that Claire felt obliged to tell her about her sins. "Once I tricked my brother into doing my chores for me because it was cold. Once I called Peter O'Brian a ninny when he said my hair looked like it'd been soaked in tomato juice. Twice I took the Lord's name in vain, but Jonny'd shoved me into a garbage heap both times, so I think that's alright." Maggie Kovak got to talk directly to God. At least that's what she told Claire, again raising her nose toward heaven like she was Mary herself.

Claire shifted a little on the kneeler, trying to get some feeling back in her toes, and wondered if the priest at Maggie's church droned on like this one, looking down his nose at the lowly sheep. His nose ran incessantly. And he stopped every couple of minutes to blow it, making a sound like a foghorn, into a yellowed handkerchief. Claire wrinkled her nose. *Ew.*

The Kovaks led very similar lives to the Ryans. Every Irish thing was just replaced by a Hungarian one. Every Catholic prayer replaced by a Protestant one. The Ryans were fresh off the boat. The Kovaks were deep into their third generation of Americanization. And Claire thought they were completely fascinating.

The décor in the Ryan house consisted of at least one icon per room and some lace that Claire's great-grandmother had hand-made and turned into a plethora of curtains and tablecloths. It was stunning. All their furniture was solid and well-kept if not of the best quality. Their home was clean, and really what more could you ask for in what would be called the "middle-class-immigrant" quarter of Chicago.

But the Kovaks had porcelain. Mrs. Kovaks grandmother had brought her Meissen figurines over on the boat with her when they immigrated, the last of the long-gone family finery. No matter how rough it got, they never sold the little figurines. When the family looked at them, they held their heads a little higher. It made them feel like they could stand in their ragged clothes before the rich and look them in the eye. The kids had ripped pictures out of magazines and tacked them to the walls. Their house was a little shabbier than the Ryan's, but it was warm. And they could pray anywhere.

The adults in the Ryan and Kovak houses had yelled at each other once and only once. It was the day they discovered they could talk about God but not religion.

Maggie Kovak's great-grandfather had left Hungary in a barrel. He had been a leader in the rebellion against the Hapsburgs. He was Protestant. Claire asked to hear the story over and over. Maggie told her Great-grandfather Kovak was chased out of Hungary by a group of Catholics with pitchforks. He arrived in America and married another Hungarian immigrant and that was the end of that. He would've been appalled that his descendants lived next door to Catholics and broke bread with the bastards to boot.

The Kovak's had a bit of land and a chicken coop, too. You could stand on the steps to each coop and talk over the little slat fence. This was one of Maggie and Claire's favorite summer pastimes before Maggie got her job. Maggie had stopped gathering the eggs when she started at the mill, so Andy took over the job. Andy had hoped the tradition of talking over the fence would continue. It didn't.

Andreas Kovak thought that Claire Ryan had the prettiest hair of any girl he'd ever seen. If he stood on the steps to the Kovak coop, he could just see her shiny red curls bouncing around over the top of the fence. When he thought about talking to her, his cheeks turned the same color as her hair.

She sang little songs that he couldn't understand as she picked up the eggs. "*Siúil, siúil, siúil a rún,*" she'd sing. "*Siúil go sochair agus siúil go ciúin.*" Her voice sounded shimmery. Like the light on the water in the brook down the hill.

Every morning Andy would sneak over to Maggie's bed and take her big warm coat off the foot of it, which made him feel silly. Then he'd comb his hair to the side, which made him feel like a man. He stood in front of the mirror and carefully opened the jar of pomade he'd bought for a nickel. If all Claire could see over the fence was his hair, then he'd make darn well sure that it looked nice.

Every day he combed his hair and peered over the fence, waiting for Claire to talk to him. And every day she sang her songs in her shimmery voice and ignored Andy completely.

"What song is that?" Andy worked up the courage to say one day. He was resting his arms on the fence and his head on his arms, looking down into the yard at Claire.

"Oh, Danny Boy," she said absentmindedly.

"I like it. It's sounds sad, though."

"It is," she said, throwing seed on the ground as the chickens pecked at her feet. "My father sings it whenever he misses the old country." She looked up at the mass of hair trying to take over the little boy's face. Andy pulled out the comb he'd stuck in his pocket and ran it over his hair. He'd seen Charlie Chaplin do this before he talked to a girl. He closed his eyes a little to make sure he looked bored. If he'd looked in a mirror, he would've seen that this didn't quite have the effect his was going for – he looked like he was about to sneeze. Claire giggled. Andy pouted, turning a bright shade of red, and ducked down behind the fence.

Claire Ryan finally started working the summer she turned twelve. The owner of the corner bookstore drank at O'Flattery's with Danny Ryan a couple nights a week, so he gave her a job shelving books and cleaning up at four dollars a week. *Four dollars a week,* she thought giddily as she skipped around the house the night before her first day.

Peggy bought her daughter a green ribbon to put in her hair.

"It looks so expensive, Ma!" Claire lightly touched the satiny ribbon in awe.

"Well, you can buy me one when you get your first dollars." She smiled in the mirror at her little girl as she tightened the ribbon around her hair.

Claire turned her head so she could see how the light reflected on the ribbon. She felt so grown up. But her mom still patted her rump as she scooted out the door, which put a temporary pout on Claire's face.

She hopped off the porch and into the summer sun and didn't quite know what to do with herself.

The door to their kitchen looked out onto the street. Danny Ryan was sitting at the kitchen table sipping his coffee and reading the morning paper. He leaned his head out the window. "You just go awalking right in the door, little Clairy and tell 'im your name. He'll do right by you." Danny had his arms crossed as he surveyed his daughter with pride plastered all over his face. He chomped on the cigar in his mouth and the Irish gleam came into his eyes.

So, she supposed, *I ought to just go awalking right in the door.*

She started down the road toward the bookstore. "Hello, Mr. O'Shanassy." She thought she'd practice on the way. "Mr. O'Shanassy! Top 'o the mornin'!" She tipped an imaginary hat. "O'Shanassy." A business-like nod. "Bryan! How's the business?" That would never do. "Hello, Mr. O'Shanassy. My name is Claire Ryan." She clicked her heels in the air, swinging her lunch pail.

She'd been in the bookstore a few times before. Her father would take her some Sundays on their way to the candy store in the Jewish corner of town. She liked the Jewish corner of town. It reminded her a lot of the Irish corner – all loud voices and loving arguments and food. Next to the candy shop, the bookstore was her favorite place in Chicago. She liked the book store's emerald green door with the gold handle – a classic Irish trick to lure a few tourists into the shop. She liked how the books smelled. And she liked the look of the different colored jackets on the shelves. *I'll organize them by color,* she thought. Then, suddenly, there was Mr. O'Shanassy, bald and round. His suspenders always looked like they were about to go on strike. His accent was even thicker than her father's; she'd always thought that was why they got along so well.

Claire swung her lunch pail back and forth gaily in contrast with the attempt at a business-like look on her face.

"Hello, Mr. O'Shanassy. I'm Claire Ryan."

Of course, not long after Claire started work, Andy Kovak suddenly developed a keen and decidedly out-of-character interest in reading. Claire counted him coming into the store almost every day.

"You really like books, huh?" she asked one day as Andy walked through the door.

"Uh, yeah! Absolutely. Nothing like some nice pieces of paper between your hands to make you feel alive, right?"

Claire watched as he turned red. "What's your favorite?"

Andy blinked. He stared at her and quickly shot his hand out to the left and grabbed a book. "This one!"

"Let me see."

He kept his eyes on her face as he walked toward her. He hesitated and reached the book across the counter, looking away as he did.

"*A Guide for Diabetics*?" She looked at the skinny boy in front of her.

"Oh…well. Yes! It's a very interesting book."

"Is it?" Claire's eyes carried the Irish light.

"Well maybe not my *favorite*, but it is very interesting." He crossed his arms and lifted his nose a fraction.

"I'll tell you my favorite book, if you like."

"Yeah?"

"Yeah. It's over there on the fiction shelf. *Little Women* by Louisa May Alcott."

"*Little Women*?"

"Yeah."

Andy put his arms on the table and rested his chin in his hands. "Does it have sword fights?"

"Sort of. There's a book inside the book that has sword fights."

He crinkled his forehead. "A book inside a book?"

"Well, you see, the main little woman is named Jo, and she writes stories, too. And all her stories have sword fights and witches and blood and guts in them."

"I wanna read that story."

"No, no. The point is that she learns to write about real people and real-life things not fairy stories."

"But I like fairy stories." He scrunched up his face then put what he thought was a very grown-up look on it. "I mean sword fight stories."

Claire liked watching his face change. It was like watching a stage actor. She smiled. "Well, this is very good for a not sword fight story. Give it a try."

"Well," Andy's hands self-consciously moved to cover his empty pockets.

"You can borrow my copy. And you could ask me any questions you had about it."

"Oh, yes! Yes." The shift happened again – first his eyes got so big they looked like two balloons on his face, ready to take his head flying away. Then he forced his face almost completely flat. Claire's Irish eyes burned brighter. *Andy Kovak is alright.*

Andy didn't sleep at all that night. He told his mother he wasn't feeling well.

"Ma, can I have my dinner in my room? My feet hurt."

"What's wrong?"

"They're tired."

"Alright, let's not make a habit of eating dinner in separate rooms, though."

"Alright. Thanks, Ma."

His mother handed him a platter instead of a plate so he wouldn't spill. He tucked the book into his coat and carried the tray with two hands up the stairs.

If he balanced the tray on his knees and held the book open with his elbow, he could eat and read at the same time. He hadn't done this much before. But he liked Jo. And Marmee reminded him of his own mother. Pretty soon he was so entranced that his potatoes had grown cold on the platter. Maggie came in.

"What on earth are you doing?"

"Huh?" He looked up from the chapter where Jo first talks to Laurie.

"You. Reading? What's wrong?" A look of mock concern spread across her face before she laughed.

"I read!"

"Since when?"

"Since always, Stupid!"

"What is it?"

"Nothing." He put the book under the platter.

"C'mon. Show me." Maggie was walking quickly toward Andy.

"No!" He doubled himself over at the waist to protect the book. "Show me!" Maggie was upon him now, tickling him furiously.

"Stop!" he gurgled through a fit of laughter. "Stop! Ma!"

"Ma!" Maggie yelled, too.

Mrs. Kovak came tramping up the stairs, dishwater dripping from her fingertips. "What on earth." She walked in on a dramatic tableau – Maggie's arm wrapped around Andy's neck, Andy clawing at Maggie's face, and the tray of potatoes perched perilously on Andy's thrashing legs. They froze as soon as they saw their mother.

"Andy won't show me what he's reading!"

"Maggie's trying to kill me!"

"Now, now. Andy, what've you got there?"

Andy dejectedly pulled *Little Women* out from under the tray of potatoes. Mrs. Kovak laughed aloud.

"You see? That's why I didn't want to show it to anyone." Andy crossed him arms and glared at his sister. She'd removed her arm from around his throat so she could point at him and laugh.

"That's a girl's book!"

"Maggie! It is not just a girl's book." Mrs. Kovak lovingly picked up the book and ran her hand across the cover. "It's a wonderful story. Andy, I'm glad you've finally taken to reading. Maggie, that reminds me – you haven't done your Bible reading for the week yet. Ten chapters, isn't it?"

Maggie shot a glare at Andy. Andy put a cold potato in his mouth and looked back at Maggie smugly, letting the half-chewed potato show through his smile. Maggie grimaced. Andy won.

The bell on the door tinkled, and Claire looked up from the box of books she was shelving. It was Andy. There were black bags under eyes, his hair was more ruffled than ever, and every single one of his shirt buttons was placed in the wrong buttonhole.

"There!" he said as he plopped the book down beside Claire. "I read every word." The light in his eyes almost rivaled the Irish.

"You read the whole thing?" Claire picked up the not-small book.

"I couldn't stop once I started."

"I told you you'd like it."

"You were right." He plopped himself down in the chair in the corner where Claire was working. "It's pretty good for a book without sword fights."

"I bet you cried when Beth died."

"Did not!"

"You did, didn't you! I can tell. Your eyes are all puffy!" Claire pointed a finger at his eyes. They were in fact very red as well as carrying handbags beneath them.

"I didn't cry. I swear! But…I…I don't know what I did. I felt it."

"Felt what?"

"What they felt."

"Who?"

"The people in the story." He gestured at the book. "They felt like my sisters."

Claire smiled. They were quiet for a while. Claire could feel Andy watching her shelve the books.

"I have an idea," Andy said after a while.

"Yeah?"

"Yeah. You give me a book to read, and I'll tell you what song you should listen to."

Claire thought about it for a minute. Andy was leaning forward in his chair, very excited. She did like music. And she really liked sharing books with people. And it didn't sound too bad to have to talk to Andy.

"Alright."

1944

They were at war.

Claire got her first pair of grown up stockings in 1942. The next day the Uncle Sam posters asking women to donate their stockings so the army could use the rayon went up around the corner. Her mom taught her how to paint seams on her legs to make it look like she had stockings on. It looked alright in the mirror but she didn't enjoy how quickly the winter air chilled her bare legs.

A lot had changed in the immigrant quarter. The echoes of the radio announcer's voice telling the people of Chicago that the Japs had just bombed Pearl Harbor hadn't dissipated by the time the police showed up outside their doors. Mrs. Pagliani a few doors down was hauled out into the street with her six children. The Paglianis went to the same parish as the Ryans. The Kovaks quietly locked their doors and closed the curtains on their windows. Italians, Japanese, Hungarians, it seemed like everyone but the Irish were being rounded up for questioning. The block grew quieter. The air grew tenser.

Claire wasn't allowed to walk alone at night anymore. To her this was a bright spot in the darkness of the war – she suddenly felt very popular with the boys. And why just walk home when you could stop by a movie first? Claire had a lot of dates in 1944. Johnny Fitzgerald, who had long since stopped picking his nose, took Claire to see the new Alfred Hitchcock movie "Lifeboat." She spent the whole day at the mill chattering about Tallulah Bankhead, the famed stage actress. She wrapped herself up in her nice wool coat, a treat bought with her own money the year before and spent half an hour arranging her fiery curls to perfectly spill over her right shoulder from under her hat. After the third coat of "Ruby Red" on her lips, she looked one last time in the mirror that was nailed sloppily to the wall in the hall at the mill and headed out into the snow.

"Gee, to be one year older!" Johnny started talking about how dumb it was to be only seventeen the moment they linked arms. "I wanna be out in the thick of it! Not sitting here collecting metal scraps like all the little kids." Claire glanced to her left, where Andy Kovak was cheerfully leading all the little kids in a "scrap parade." He blew on his whistle every evening when he got home from work, and all the kids on the block came running through the snow to his front door.

"Attention!" Andy shouted, and the children fell into line. The girls' braids bounced around as they ran across the streets. The boys made a game of tying the girls' braids together when they weren't watching. She turned away to hide her grin. *Some things never change.* Johnny was muttering something about how silly it was to be in America when you could be in Europe "shitting on the Germans." But Andy didn't look silly. Claire thought he looked sort of noble. His glance met hers as he bent down to pick up a can from the snowy ground. There was a little boy hanging off his back pointing forward and shouting "Charge!"

"You know?" Johnny asked. Claire nodded her head and thought about how nice it would be to talk about something other than the war. It wasn't that she didn't understand the importance of it. Or that she didn't feel for the GI's. She did. *It'll be nice to see a movie.*

There were twenty minutes of war footage before the film started. That meant twenty minutes of Johnny asking her how old he looked, wondering if he could pass for an older boy. The film was about an extremely unlikely group of people traveling by sea to Europe who end up on a lifeboat after their ship has been hit by a German U-boat. There was a "Buy War Bonds" add at the end of it.

Tallulah Bankhead didn't disappoint. But the highlight had been when one of the characters was revealed as the captain of the U-boat that had hit them. Claire had her hands on the edge of her seat to keep from falling out of it. The film was reflected on the tears streaming down her cheeks.

She went out and tried to sell her wool coat the next day.

"Claire! What in God's name are you doing?" Peggy Ryan crossed herself for her daughter's madness and grabbed the coat from Claire.

"They're over on the front dying so I can sit in a warm theatre in my nice coat. It's the least I can do."

"Hang on, Clairy. There are steps ye can take before you sell the shirt off yer back. What good are you to the soldiers if you're frozen into a block of ice?"

Claire kept her coat and wore it on the way to ask Mr. O'Shannassy if she could turn the bookstore into a bandage wrapping station after hours. O'Shannassy let her fill a corner in the shop with a few chairs and a table. She put all the medical books in that corner and got together a group of her friends. If Andy Kovak could carry little kids around in a snowstorm collecting metal for the boys, then she certainly could do her part. The window now read "O'Shannassy's Books," and underneath there was a little hand painted piece of paper reading "Ryan's Wrappings: Volunteers Wanted!"

Maggie Kovak showed up at five every day as the shop was closing with her kid siblings' red wagon overflowing with cloth. The rest of the volunteer girls trickled in as they got off from the mills.

"They say our boys are stronger than ever." Maggie was appointed to read the newspaper at the start of every session. She tried to pick out the most hopeful phrases in the articles. Maybe twisted a few words to make it sound nicer. This was a habit she'd taken up after the first couple of meetings. She had mentioned a lost battle that was on the front page at the first meeting, and the girl to her right cringed. She had brothers at the front.

They tried to be political and discuss what Mr. Churchill was doing for the Allies in England and what theatres the local boys had ended up in. But they only knew so much about things like that. And they could only stomach so much information about the wounds their bandages would cover. The conversation inevitably drifted to happier things as their fingers flew over the bandages.

"Application season is coming up," Maggie said at the beginning of one of the meetings as she folded up the paper and set it on the table without reading a word from it. Claire glanced across the table at it and flipped it over quickly. The front page was a full picture of two teenage boys. They were waist deep in mud, one was bleeding from his head. The other was dragging him to safety. Claire swallowed and flipped the paper back over.

"Where are you gonna go?" asked a smallish girl with round glasses, scrunched eyes, and even more scrunched curls.

"I'm thinking of Northwestern." Claire got it into her head that college was where life really began. As their fingers flew over bandages, this group of friends had bonded together over a singular desire – to leave the immigrant quarter.

Andy used his allowance to buy a cap gun. Now his morning routine included grabbing the gun and practice-marching around the house before work. He hummed "Don't Sit Under the Apple Tree" and saluted himself in the mirror by the door, slid his hand across his hat brim and spun around, popping the collar on his jacket. He felt quite spiffy. Although he looked a little more like a singing coat rack than Errol Flynn.

He walked to work every morning at dawn. By now he'd passed off egg duty to one of the younger kids. He was proud of his job. The mill he worked at manufactured steel. As he worked, he pictured all the things he was creating by supplying steel. *Guns for our boys, cars for our boys.*

There were twelve Uncle Sam posters on the walls of the buildings between his house and the mill. And every "I want you!" dug straight into his chest. No one in his family was fighting. He was the oldest boy and still far too young, and his father was marked 4F on account of his high arches. But there were those twelve Uncle Sams, each one's eyes boring into Andy's soul. That's why he started collecting metal scraps. That's why he took his record collection, his prized record collection, down to the scrap drive for shellac. If he was honest with himself, he would've rather collected scraps on his lunch break in the daylight. But Claire Ryan wasn't out on a date with some guy during his lunch break.

Claire's date with Johnny was the second one she'd been on that week, and merely the next in a long succession of dates this winter. Andy had seen her come and go almost every time. He really, *really* didn't want to be some creepy guy that couldn't stop watching her...But every time she went on a date, he worried about her.

He'd figured out that if he left the mill five minutes later than normal, he could sometimes catch her on her way home. If he did this, then she didn't need anyone else to walk with her.

At night before he went to bed he examined himself in his sister's handheld mirror. *Grow, dammit.* He ran his hand over his chin. Patchy. Unconvincing. His best friend Tommy Lansing had tried it. Tommy had walked right up to the enlistment office and said, "Sign me up, Sarge!" The sergeant had looked up from his forms at the scrawny kid standing brazenly in his office. "We just got twenty boxes of toothpicks in last week, son. Won't need any more for a while." Andy, listening by the door covered his mouth and snickered. Tommy hung his head and walked out. "Shut up," Tommy said to Andy as he left the office.

Andy skipped up behind Johnny. "Been neglecting your spinach lately, Tommy?"

"I said shut up."

Andy burst out into a rousing chorus of "When Johnny Comes Marching Home Again," and Tommy chased him down the road trying to get close enough to sock him in the jaw.

Andy had a nice voice. People always told him he sounded like a kid Bing Crosby – his voice a little bit higher but still with that buttery sound.

It seemed wrong to be celebrating during the war. When she saw the big envelope plopped on her doorstep, Claire stood stock still. There was a big seal stamped to the front of it: "Northwestern." She blinked. Her hands flew to the envelope of their own accord, tearing the thing open frantically.

"Dear Miss Ryan," she closed her eyes and breathed in.

"Congratulations." She ran inside shouting. "Congratulations! Ma, it says congratulations!"

The battle was no longer in Europe. It was no longer between the Americans and the Germans. It was at Northwestern. And it was between Claire and algebra.

"Why in God's name does an English teacher need to know anything about math?" She was covering her face with her hands. She'd been sinking lower and lower in her chair during the last hour. She now sat perilously on the edge, her head leaned all the way against the back of the chair. It was the first day of class and she already had two pages of equations to get through.

"Why don't you go take a walk?" Maggie was buried deep in her own studies.

"I don't wanna walk. I wanna be done."

Maggie glanced up from her work at Claire. "Then I'm going for a walk."

"Don't leave me alone with this!" Claire put on a mock pout.

Maggie put on her jacket. "You're fine."

"Ugh, fine." Claire untangled herself from her chair, with great difficulty, and walked to the kitchen. Her fuzzy socks slid across the tile. She liked this. She stuck her arms out on either side of her and slid, moving her arms like wings.

"Do your homework." Maggie ducked out the door into the cold.

"I'm gonna learn how to make crème brulee first!" Claire shouted at the closing door. Outside, Maggie looked back through the kitchen window and shook her head at Claire. Claire stuck out her tongue and put the kettle on to boil. She caught a glimpse of her reflection in the shiny yellow range hood. She looked like an escaped convict. *Yikes.* She went back to her room to at least wash her face.

She was sitting on the table munching on cookies and decidedly ignoring her homework while she waited for the water to boil when she heard a knock. A loud knock. A really loud knock.

She put her cookie down and brushed the crumbs off her lips. She looked through the peep hole. She saw an enormous forehead. Whoever it was looked like the alien thing she'd seen at the movies. *The Monster Man? Monster and the Lady? Lady Monster? Doesn't matter.* She looked down to see what she was wearing – night gown, robe, fuzzy socks. She glanced around her for a minute. *Coat.*

"Hello?" Claire called through the door.

"University looks good on you."

Claire squinted as she opened the door. "Andy?"

"Who the heck did you think I was? Doing well I see." He was laughing at her. She could feel it. She could also hear it, which made her thoroughly convinced that he found her outfit, mussed hair and makeup, and obvious lack of caffeination funny. She narrowed her eyes.

"Hey, I have all A's. If this is how I have to look to get there, then so be it." She pulled her coat a little tighter around her and smoothed her hand over her hair, obviously going for a Carol Lombard look of superiority. Andy laughed and she smiled. "Come in?"

"Yeah, you want some coffee?"

"I'm supposed to offer that." She walked back into the kitchen and filled the kettle again.

"You look like you need it more than I do." There was that face again. That Andy Kovak face. Smug then sweet; childlike then serious. She never knew what to make of that. But it made her laugh.

"You're a wonderful guest you know that? What brings you to town anyway? Big business deal?" She leaned against the stove and crossed her arms. She hadn't seen him in months. Maggie said he'd been wandering a bit since the end of the war.

"Deciding what I want to do this weekend. The campus directory said my options are a two-hour clarinet recital or a dissection demonstration. Thoughts?"

"Really."

"The dissection flyer said that people with weak stomachs weren't invited."

"Andy."

He sat down on the table and put his hands in his pockets. "I'm studying."

"What?" She jumped forward off the stove as the kettle started screeching. "Studying what?"

"Music."

"Really?" She turned around to face him. *Music.* She hadn't thought about their little book and record club in she couldn't remember how long.

He looked at her. "Nothing?"

"What do you mean?"

"No mocking?"

"No! Why would I mock you?"

"Maggie, the girl, is here studying to be a doctor, and her kid brother throws away his family's money on becoming a canary."

Claire liked watching his eyes. They lit up just as quickly as the light could fall out of them. It happened in that one sentence. Between the word money and canary, he'd gone from a lighthouse to a match.

She crossed her arms and leaned against the stove again. "I say follow your heart."

"That's disgusting."

Claire heard the lock being jiggled. "Maggie!" Claire turned around as she was opening the door. "I found your brother." She put her hand to the side of her mouth, looking at Andy, and whispered, "And I might strangle him."

"What did he ever do to you?" Maggie was laughing.

"He was almost as stressful as algebra."

"I heard that. And I'm sorry, but I had to see my little sister." Andy was patting Maggie's head as he spoke. Despite being two years older than he was, Maggie was now almost a foot shorter than him.

He stayed for a few hours. It turned out Maggie had known he was coming to school in the fall, she'd just forgotten to tell Claire. He had decided to study music after the fifteenth time someone had told him he sounded like a young Bing Crosby. Fifteen is too many times to be told anything not to try it. He'd been wandering a bit since the war. Unlike the rest of the boys experiencing this sense of displacement, Andy's purposelessness stemmed from *not* having fought. He felt inferior to all the other boys around his age. He hadn't done anything.

"I started working at O'Flattery's just to get away from all the stories."

"And how'd that work out for you?" Claire had spent enough time at the corner pub to know that stories were bred in the stout and the darkness.

"It sounds like you know." Andy looked over his tea at Claire. She had started studying the moment she took off her coat. Her comments came hazily from in between equations. "I didn't escape the stories, but I found music. It started as a joke. I'd lead the men in drinking songs. But then one day Mr. O'Flattery told me my Hungarian tone didn't sound too bad on the Irish tunes. He asked me to sing 'Oh Danny Boy.'"

Claire stopped chewing on her pencil eraser. "I love that song."

"I know."

She looked back down at her algebra. He looked down at her.

"Well, I really should be getting back." He awkwardly put down his tea and slid his chair back from the table.

Maggie reached up to hug her brother.

"It was good seeing you again, Andy." Claire stood up from the table and reached out her hand.

"You, too, Claire."

Andy shut the door to Claire and Maggie's room behind him and stood on the front steps. A smile crept across his face. He clicked his heels and jumped off the steps. He whistled all the way back to his room on the other side of the campus. He didn't tell Claire that he'd learned all the Irish tunes he sang in the pub from listening to her sing at the chicken coop.

He'd realized in O'Flattery's that he not only liked singing, he had to sing. The first night he'd sung at the pub, he'd immediately gone home and started hammering away at the old family spinet.

"Andy, Ma's been trying to teach you for ten years, and I think this is the first time I've ever heard you practice without a ruler hovering over your hands."

He'd turned around to see Maggie leaning against the door of the parlor with a smirk on her face.

In the two days since he'd come to the university, he'd spent a total of zero daylight hours outside of the conservatory. He'd never seen so many instruments. He sat at the piano and sang, snuck into the concert hall to practice singing with the acoustics. He even picked up a tuba and gave a few blows. It was heaven.

In the course of his exploration, he'd also found the record room. It was a small room, about the size of the practice rooms in the conservatory, and every inch of it was covered in records. A little Victrola sat in the corner on top of a few crates of records. This was his favorite room.

"Alright, alright." Claire was annoying Maggie again. Claire untangled herself from the chair, with great difficulty, and walked to the coat rack. "If I'm not back in thirty minutes, 'I've thrown meself into the sea.'" Claire smiled at her joke. How many times had her father used that exact phrase when he was frustrated?

Maggie laughed and made a shooing motion with her hand.

Out in the crisp fall air, Claire stopped to breathe deeply and stretched her arms above her head. She glanced to her right over towards the campus dining hall. There were maple trees with falling leaves and crumpled papers blowing across the sidewalk. Then she looked to her left towards the way into the town. There were shiny cars and paper boys and hat shops and book stores. She pulled her coat collar up higher on her neck, shoved her hands in her pockets, and trudged left.

She wore her hair differently now – a little shorter and pin-curled in the front. She wasn't one of the fancy girls at school. She wore coarser fabric and couldn't afford the nice things they had. She didn't look as nice, but she was prettier than all of them. Not necessarily because of her features or her figure; she was objectively lovely, but there were other girls with more curved noses and hips. She was beautiful because of how she carried herself. She was conscious of her differences, and she wasn't ashamed. She was proud of her family. She was proud of the little lilt she had in her speech. She was proud of her undeniably Irish red hair. She wore herself well.

Claire Ryan had another difference. She had a job. Mr. O'Shannassy knew a nice Irishman who ran a bookstore near Claire's college, and he got her a job there. Other girls looked down on Claire because she worked. But Claire felt lucky.

She headed toward town. Over the past three years, she'd gotten to know the area pretty well, and she thought she'd go down to Mrs. Mitchell's dress shop.

"We're getting a lot of new styles in, you know, for the winter." Mrs. Mitchell always wore her hair in a tight but flattering knot at the back of her head and had a tape measure forever thrown around her neck like a scarf. "Tempted?" she'd asked Claire a couple days before.

Claire rummaged through her coat pockets now. *Gum wrapper, ticket stub, pencil, two dollars.* She stopped. *Two dollars.* Maybe not. She turned back around and walked toward the dining hall. She stopped in front of the campus directory. "Roommate wanted," "Dissection demonstration for prospective agricultural students (please do not attend if you have a weak stomach)," "Clarinet concert at music hall this Friday!" etc.

Andy spent two hours getting ready. Two hours. This was only possible because he was at school. This was the first time in his life that he had shared more than one toilet, shower, and sink. He still shared of course. But there were so many options! The mere fact that he didn't have to spend fifteen minutes banging on the door just to get into the bathroom seemed like Heaven. He'd brought a little hand mirror and a bowl for shaving, expecting to have to do most of his day-to-day ablutions in his room. But no – it might be a smidge crowded, but all twenty boys in his hall could get ready at the same time if they wanted to. And they frequently did. 4:02 on a Friday night was a very popular time to get spiffy. Andy didn't want to go the clarinet concert or to the dissection. But he had an idea.

This Friday, every boy was talking about their date.

"Amy's got quite the figure."

"What a dame!"

"You see Mary's red dress?"

"And that Claire! Hair like Maureen O'Hara."

Andy paused, his shaving cream brush in the air. He looked at his ghostly face in the mirror – like a banana cream pie. He ran the razor slowly, meticulously across his face. One stroke, *He doesn't mean anything by it.* Second stroke, *Her eyes have gotten even greener.* Third stroke, *Maybe I'll ask the boys about the best joints.* He swished his razor under the water. "Hey fellas?" Ten heads turned toward him. "Where's the best place to take a girl around here?"

"Oh, the movies. Obviously."

"Yeah, nice and dark."

Andy looked at them. "But then you can't see her."

"And no one can see you either, if you know what I mean." All the boys in the room whooped and hollered.

Andy turned back to the mirror. He probably wouldn't ask the boys for anymore suggestions. A picture of a group of monkeys grooming themselves would be an accurate comparison in this instance in both sight and sound. You could crack walnuts on their hair. Each one's head was choked up with pomade like shellac.

"There's a nice burger joint on 2ⁿᵈ." The blond boy next to him paused in his shaving to talk. "And there's dancing next door for fifty-five cents apiece. Don't listen to them." The boy raised his voice a little and said, "They've never gotten a girl to talk to them for any reason other than a free meal."

A bunch of guffaws rose up from around the sinks. "You're not doing so hot either, Casanova."

Another said, "Wanna bet, Bobby?"

Andy smiled and chuckled. "Thanks for the tip. I'm Andy." He extended a wet, shaving cream covered hand. The blond guy did the same.

"Bobby Crawley. Pleasure."

They went back to shaving quietly as the boys around them got rowdier and rowdier.

Andy called Claire at five exactly.

"Hey. It's Andy."

"Oh, hi, Andy." He thought he could hear pages rustling.

"I have a proposition."

"Which is?" It sounded like a book slammed shut.

"You meet me at the music hall, and I'll show you what I found. Bring your favorite book you've read recently, too. It'll be just like when we were kids."

The line was quiet for a second. He jiggled the coin insert a couple times. "Claire?"

"Yeah, I was thinking. That sounds great. I can't look at this stuff another second anyway."

"Great!" He hung up the phone. He stood staring at it for a minute before clicking his heels again.

Claire had gotten three calls just that night for dates. She'd said an emphatic, but charming, "no" to everyone. She'd gone through the boy-crazy phase during the war. All the other girls were just entering it in college. She was over the need to have a date every night in order to feel special. She would much rather eat at the dining hall with Maggie or a good book than waste her time staring at a greasy loud-mouth just to get a free burger.

As she hung up the phone, she thought, *Claire, you idiot.* And in some ways, she was right – she surveyed the mountain of homework she had to get through before the next week started. She could always skip the movie and come back to do homework. Every date was the same. Dinner. Movie. Dinner. Movie. Sometimes there was the added adventure of fending off unwanted and awkwardly advanced kisses. She was a master of the "Well, goodnight!" dodge, opening the car door and jumping out right as some guy was leaning in. The boys didn't mean anything by it, and she never felt like she was in danger. She just wasn't particularly interested in any of them.

She looked at herself in the mirror by the door. *Not bad. Not great.* She mussed her hair and looked again. She was wearing a very scholastic plaid skirt with a burgundy sweater. Her hair was slightly contained with the green satin ribbon her mom had given her the day she got her job at the mill. She wore it as a headband now – more hip. The red hair frizzing up into a cloud behind the headband made her look like a chrysanthemum. *Whatever.*

She grabbed her purse and ran out the door. "Bye, Maggie. I'll be back soon."

"Where you going?"

Claire stopped in the doorway. "I'm going out with your brother."

Maggie's jaw dropped. Claire winked at Maggie and flung open the door before Maggie had a chance to say anything.

She closed the door behind her and stopped short at the top of the stairs. "Oh, hey." She was face to face with Andy.

"Hey. I was walking by anyway, so I figured I'd wait for you." Andy looked up, smiling from the bottom of the stairs. He looked like a kid again standing there so far below her.

Across campus, a boy howled. "Great! Protect me from the wolves," Claire said as she hopped down the stairs, smiling too, and took the elbow Andy offered. She noticed that his face matched her hair. Maybe it was just the reflection of the setting sun. He had a huge bag in his other hand.

"What's that?"

"I grabbed us some burgers from that place on 2nd." He raised the bag a little like it was a prized animal he'd hunted down on a safari.

"Good thinking. I'm starving!" She reached for the bag. He yanked it out of reach.

"Not yet! I've got an idea."

The music hall was only a few yards away. He led her through the side doors. She winced as a screeching clarinet came wafting in from the auditorium.

"Up here." Andy threw open a narrow door, displaying a steep staircase. It was dark and looked like the kind of staircase that would lead up to an attic where someone would keep their nutty wife.

"Ah, I get it now."

"What?"

"You're murdering me."

Andy laughed. She'd never noticed his laugh before. Come to think of it, she wasn't sure she'd heard it much since his voice had deepened. She suddenly thought she knew why. His laugh sounded like it'd been left behind in puberty – his voice was a warm, almost chocolaty baritone, but his laugh had a hyena-like quality. She laughed, too.

"I know," Andy said, stopping on the stairs in front of her.

"You know what?"

"My laugh. I hate my laugh."

"No! It's nice. I mean yeah it makes you sound a bit like Mickey Mouse, but it's contagious." She smiled at him mischievously.

He laughed again. Her smile broadened, and she laughed, too.

"So if you're not locking me in the attic with Edward Rochester's wife, then what is this?"

He'd started to climb the stairs without her and was disappearing into the dark. "You'll see. I told you I wanted to show you what I'd found. I figure you've been at school long enough to start feeling like a real grownup, and what fun is that? I thought we'd have a real kid-like adventure for a change." His eyes twinkled when he turned around to look at her.

"Anything to get away from algebra."

They were suddenly at the top of the staircase. It was a very narrow top landing scrunched up against a door. Andy balanced the bag of burgers on his knee as he leaned against the door. "Ready?"

"Yeah."

He shoved his weight against the door three times, and it burst open, letting in a brisk autumn breeze.

"Whew, that's cold." Claire wrapped her arms around her torso before stepping out the door.

"Ta-da!" Andy waved his arms with a flourish and a smile like he'd just pulled off an astounding magic trick.

"We're on the roof?"

"Yep! Look." He pointed. "You can see all the way downtown."

"Where's that music coming from?"

"Ah, yes, excellent question, Miss Ryan." He pushed a pair of imaginary glasses up his nose. "That would be coming from the hall of music below us."

She tilted her head and smirked at him. "Well, I know that. But I mean it like 'Yay, it's not a screeching clarinet.'"

"Yeah, that's cause we're standing on top of the practice rooms. Someone must be playing piano."

Claire turned her whole body all the way around, taking it in. "You know, I think this is the highest above the ground I've ever been."

He plopped himself on the gravel ground and pulled the burgers out of the bag. "Sit down here so you don't fall off. We'll eat quick, ok? We've got more on the itinerary."

"Aren't Maggie and I supposed to be the ones showing *you* around?"

"Simple. You aren't explorers like I am." His mouth was full of cheeseburger. "Non-explorers make terrible tour-guides."

Claire sat down beside him and unwrapped her burger. "So can I ask you something?"

Andy smiled through the burger. "Yeah."

"Have you made many friends yet?" She glanced over at him hesitantly.

Andy laughed. "Nah."

"Nah? That's it?"

Andy finished chewing before he answered. "No. I don't know. It's only been a week.

I'm not good at talking to new people." He took another contemplative bite. "There's this one guy, Bobby, I met."

"That's good. I don't know what I would've done here without Maggie. It's hard to move to a new place and not know anyone."

"But I know you."

Claire smiled. "True! And Maggie."

"Eh."

Claire's laugh got strangled by her burger. "Eh? C'mon. You and your sister are close."

"Yeah, but she's my sister." He faked nausea. "Anyway, ready for the next adventure?"

Claire popped the last bite of burger into her mouth. Claire grabbed the hand Andy extended and pulled herself up. She brushed off her skirt and gave a thumbs up. "Let's go."

Andy pirouetted and leaped back toward the door. Claire laughed and shook her head. "You're strange, Andy Kovak."

"Hurry up!"

Claire sighed in mock frustration and twirled toward him smiling.

Her hair made an Irish halo around her head as she twirled, her green eyes flashing at his every time her head whipped back around. She looked like a wood-sprite, like joy itself. Andy looked away and hurried down the stairs before she could see his face. He was entranced.

Honestly, he was lonely. Growing up with eight siblings makes some people prefer quiet and time alone. It made Andy hate being alone. From some fluke, he'd ended up the only guy on his floor in a room by himself. Not having a roommate wore on him. He'd never had a room to himself. Not in all his life. He found he couldn't sleep without someone snoring on the opposite side of the room. He hated looking over at the empty bed across from him. His brother, or at least another student, should be there. He couldn't stand it. It was great to have Maggie there, but she almost made things worse. She re-minded him too much of home to be comforting. Every time he saw her, he just wanted his mom. But he was a man. He couldn't say things like that.

But Claire. She was the perfect mix. One – he had been madly in love with her since he could walk. And two – she reminded him of home without making him wish he was there. She brought home to him. And she liked his laugh.

He wanted a friend. And there one was, twirling toward him with that bewitching smile.

He ran down the stairs. "Hurry up!" he called up the stairs. He heard heels pounding dangerously fast down the steps. He smiled. "Don't die!" he added.

She slid to a stop in front of him breathlessly. "Ta-da!" she mimicked his hand gesture from before.

"C'mon!" he grabbed her hand and yanked her through the door.

"I can't catch my breath."

"Don't be a pansy."

"Where are we going now?"

"Would it be an adventure if you knew?"

"No."

"Exactly. You're welcome."

"For what?"

"You'll see." He stopped her suddenly. They were in front of another little door. He jiggled the handle. He threw his hip against the door. He stopped, looked at Claire, and sighed.

Claire folded her arms and leaned against the wall. "You could've picked rooms with working doors, you know."

"What's the," he jiggled the handle, "fun," he pushed against the door with his palms, "in that?" he hip-checked it again and the door fell inward, making Andy stumble forward.

Claire giggled and slipped past him into the room, tipping an imaginary hat as she glid by. She felt the walls for the light switch, flicked it on, and gasped. "Wow."

"I know!" Andy was standing in front of piles and piles of records, beaming.

"How'd you find this?"

"Curiosity." He was rifling through the boxes, picking up and blowing the dust off of records as he went. He held up a copy of a Billie Holliday record. "Welcome to the archive room – every record the university owns. Fun fact, I've even found some by the students."

"What?"

"Yeah! They've got a studio downstairs. I plan to have gone platinum by the time I graduate." He waggled his eyebrows.

"Oh, wow. The Andrews Sisters!" Claire was holding up an entire box.

"They've got a few crates of Bing Crosby, too."

"Oh! *Gershwin plays Gershwin*!" She was clutching it to her chest.

"You like Gershwin?"

"'Rhapsody in Blue' is my favorite piece of all time."

"But Gershwin was Jewish."

"Wow, racist."

"No, no. I mean he's not Irish."

Claire was smiling at him and sitting on the edge of some crates, her arms crossed. "Again. Racist."

He threw his hands in the air and laughed. "No! I mean the only thing I ever heard you sing were Irish tunes."

"Exactly how does one go about singing 'Rhapsody in Blue?'"

"Like this." He started humming the end section of the song, waving his hands around wildly as he conducted his imaginary orchestra. He even crashed together imaginary cymbals.

Claire threw her head back when she laughed. It made her hair bounce around every which way, shining as it did. He started laughing, too.

"I concede. It's possible. But not easy," Claire said.

"'Danny Boy' is nice, too."

They sifted through the archives for over an hour, pausing every time one of them found something interesting. They'd found a record with the name "Lloyd's Love Songs for Lunatic Lovers." They listened to that while they browsed.

"*Lady love…how…how…*" Lloyd was having trouble. "*Lady love…you…bitch.*" Lloyd was decidedly drunk. Claire had laughed so hard she cried when Lloyd let out the slurred slur.

"Who let them put this in here?" Claire could barely speak.

"I've got a theory – Lloyd gets his heart broken by a girl, right, so he goes out and buys a few cases of beer for himself and his buddies. They get the bright idea they're gonna break into the studio, they're music majors of course, and record what Lloyd thinks is a heartbreaking record detailing his recently ended romance. They sobered up and put it in here as a prank."

"Poor Lloyd," Claire said as she wiped tears off her cheeks and tried to catch her breath.

"We've all been there."

"*Shit,*" said Lloyd. There was a clanking of bottles as he clearly stumbled around the studio singing.

Claire and Andy doubled over laughing.

"Alright, let's put Lloyd out of his misery. Time for the next adventure."

"What time is it?"

Andy covered the face of his watch with his other hand. "Does it matter?"

Claire thought for a second. "No. No, it doesn't."

Claire quietly opened the door to her apartment at what she later discovered was midnight. The last part of the adventure had been sneaking into the auditorium, the clarinet concert was long over, and sitting at the piano. Claire closed the door to her apartment and leaned against it, remembering.

"One second." Andy had left her standing in the dark on the stage. A second later, the spotlight blinded her.

"Ow!"

"Sorry!" His voice was muffled from the wings of the stage. He came back to the piano and sat down. He stood back up and brushed his imaginary tailcoats behind him and ran his hand through his hair dramatically. Claire giggled.

She giggled now while she remembered, too. She dropped her bag and let herself sink to the floor at the foot of the door. She smiled.

He'd raised his hands high above the piano like he was preparing to play a Franz Liszt Consolation. His hands fell to the keys. "*Don't sit under the apple tree with anyone else but me, anyone else but me, anyone else but me.*" He scooped the last note and did the whole thing in falsetto.

Claire burst out laughing and came to sit beside him. He sat facing the piano, and she sat facing away, turning her head to watch his face as he played.

Now, Claire hummed the song to herself as she got up from the door and slipped into her bedroom.

It is important at this point for the reader to become aware – all was not as right between the Kovaks and the Ryans as the children had been led to believe. Perhaps a sense of security has been achieved in these last chapters. Claire and Andy are feeling it, too. Of course, they, unlike the readers, don't have the benefit of knowing their futures. But be warned – this is not all black and white, the Andrews Sisters, and laugh tracks. It all began when the Ryans invited the Kovaks to dinner. During Lent.

1933

"We've given up alcohol, Danny."

Danny paused mid-pour and looked up at his wife. "Right. Sorry, Peggy." He screwed the cap back on the stout with a look of regret. "You know how it is, Jósef, first day of Lent." He winked at his guest.

"I didn't know it was Lent." Jósef Kovak looked confused.

"Well, what did you give up?"

"I'm Protestant. Thought you were, too."

Danny paused. "You think I'm Protestant?"

"I think you're Irish, and come to think of it, I guess that's the same thing as Catholic."

Danny let out a jolly laugh. "The Ryans have been Catholic for an age. We're not joining the bloody Ulsters now."

Jósef Kovak's face had an uncanny resemblance to stone. "Protestantism is not a joke, Mr. Ryan."

"I wasn't laughing at the Protestants, Mr. Kovak, I was laughing at the accusation of being one."

"Do you have any idea what your people did to mine?"

"Preserved Christianity for a few thousand years? Yes, sir. And proud of it."

Mr. Kovak's voice was quiet and grave as he said, "Your bastard ideological relatives drove my father out of Hungary with pitchforks."

"Watch your tongue, sir. You may think less of me, but in this Christian home, we don't use that language. That's pub language." Danny's eyes lit a bit. It was a mix of fires – half the red of anger, half the white of humor.

"I am not in a joking mood, Mr. Ryan."

Danny stared Jósef up and down. The Hungarian was a tall, lean man with a black beard and disproportionately large eyebrows. The eyebrows were sewn together above his eyes at the moment, achieving an effect that was both intimidating and reminiscent of a caterpillar. Danny crossed his arms and said, "Perhaps this wasn't the best idea, our getting together."

"I agree." József stood and brushed off his hat that had been sitting in his lap. "Come along, Maria." His wife looked at Peggy in dismay. She seemed almost ashamed. Peggy glanced at her own husband. They never did anything, including leaving dinner at a neighbor's, without quite a bit of debate, which always came with many "My dears" and "Love of my lifes" to ease the tension. The Ryans were known, like many Irish couples, for showing their love in arguments. All in all, it was a very different marriage than that of the Kovaks. And a very different household than that of the Kovaks. Maria gathered the children and the Kovaks were gone.

1948

"Ma, you'll never guess who Andy's been hanging around." Maggie twirled the phone cord around her finger.

"Oh, who? I've been praying the Lord would bring him some friends." Maria's voice still had the crystal quality it had had when Maggie was a little girl. Clear and lovely like crystal, but with every one of its sharp edges.

"Claire Ryan!"

"Claire?" Maria, who'd been prepared to smile, faltered.

"Yeah! Isn't it wonderful! The three of us friends like when we were kids."

"Hm, wonderful." Maria loved Claire. She did. She loved that Maggie had been able to have the same friend her whole life. Maria knew her daughter needed that stability. And Claire was a good girl. Claire was fine as Maggie's friend. But it was not fine that Claire was sniffing around her son.

"You look fantastic. C'mon!" Andy was flipping through the pages of Claire's math homework.

Claire came out of the bathroom with her hands in her hair, fluffing up her already lion-like mane. "Pipe down. If I'm going to the symphony, I'm going looking my best." She'd ditched the ever-present green ribbon in her hair for an all-down look.

She checked the effect in the mirror and saw Andy looking at her in the reflection. "What?"

"Nothing. I just had no idea."

"No idea about what?"

"No idea that I was going out with Rita Hayworth." He put down the homework, stood up, and came close behind her.

"You idiot." She looked at herself again with a smirk. She did look nice. She ran her hands through her curls one more time. "Alright," she turned towards him. "What do you think?"

He twirled her around. "Can I call you Gilda?"

Claire hit him playfully on the chest. "Let's go."

It was warm now. The chill of the Illinois winter had passed, leaving behind a world scrubbed clean of the previous year. New earth, new blooms, new life. The breeze coming through the beat-up car's window played with Claire's curls. She closed her eyes and smiled as she felt the air brush through her eyelashes and glide over her cheeks, leaving a pale pink on them.

Claire turned to Andy. "What do you know about this Kopek fellow who's conducting?"

"Not much, except that he sounds like a mighty fine man."

"'Cause his name sounds Hungarian?"

"You betcha'." Andy winked.

Claire rolled her eyes and reached her hand over to rub Andy's shoulders as he drove.

"Rhapsody in Blue" had been perfect. Andy looked over at Claire, and she was perfect. He looked at his beat-up jalopy, and it was perfect. The burger he was inhaling as he drove was perfect.

He pulled the car over to the side of the road. They'd reached an overlook. From here, you could see above the city, all the lights of it, the bustle.

"Why are we stopping?" Claire looked content and confused.

"Another adventure." Andy stretched into the back of the car. "I thought, if I'm going out with Rita Hayworth, I'd better wine and dine her." He presented Claire with an enormous smile, a bottle of club soda, and some cheese and crackers.

"You idiot." She smiled with more of her face than anyone he'd ever seen. It was like even her ears were happy.

"And that's not all this idiot brought for you."

"Where are you going?"

He jumped out of the car and opened the trunk. There was a lot of clanking and clattering, and then suddenly there was a scratching sound and then music. "Rhapsody in Blue."

"How on earth are you doing that?" Claire opened her door and leaned her head around to the back.

"Ta da!" He showed off his ingenious addition to the day – in the trunk of his car sat a wind-up Victrola.

Claire's jaw dropped. "Where'd you get that?"

He held his finger to his lips in response.

"From the music hall?"

"Maybe."

"Andy!"

"What? No one goes in there but you and me anyway."

"Thief!" She ran up to him and tackled him. Or tried to. In reality, she just ended up hanging from his neck.

He couldn't stop laughing his hyena laugh as he set her down on the ground. He bowed to her gracefully as the music swelled from his trunk.

"Won't we wake people up?" Claire looked around her as she took the hand he offered her.

"Claire. We're in the middle of nowhere."

"Right." She stared up at him as they began to dance under the stars.

"I know I'm strange, but I thought it'd be fun."

"You're not strange, you're Peter Pan."

They were quiet for a while, the music swelling to fill the happy silence. Claire noticed Andy look away from her when she tried to meet his gaze. "What's wrong?"

"I just." He stopped and looked away.

"Andy." Her hand turned his face toward her again.

"Fine." He huffed. "I just feel like. I feel like there's something I should tell you."

"Yes?"

He stopped dancing. "I love you."

She looked up at him and put her hand on his cheek. His eyes lit up, and he bent down to kiss her.

"Mom."

"And the Pattersons next door keep going on and on about the noise – "

"Mom."

"And I don't understand why, when they scream at each other 'til midnight every night, it's a problem that my children play – "

"Ma!"

"Oh, sorry, Clairy. You know how I get. All worked up and couldn't stop. What is it, dear?"

"I have something to tell you." Claire was sitting on her couch in her apartment. She could picture her mom perfectly – little silk floral head scarf keeping the dust off of her hair while she cleaned. She'd never seen an Irish woman look more like a French maid than her mom.

"Oh, did you get an A in math?"

"Ma, that'd take God putting a pencil in his hand and taking the exam for me."

"And I've been praying for just that."

Claire rested her forehead on her hand and wrapped the phone cord around her fingers.

"Ma, Andy's in love with me."

"Oh! My dear, with who?"

"Andy Kovak. With me." There was silence. "Ma?" More silence. More silence than there had ever been in any conversation with her mother. "Ma!"

"Claire, he isn't Catholic."

"So what?"

"Claire, it isn't done."

"Ma. This is 1948. It's America."

"I know what year it is, dear." Her tone had hardened. Mrs. Ryan had most likely set down her feather duster, which she used unironically, and very quietly uncorked the scotch. It was three. She was allowed to drink after three.

"Exactly! Those things don't matter anymore."

"I pray you don't believe that." Peggy's voice was stone-cold.

"But *why* would it matter?"

"Do you have any idea what his people did to ours?" Peggy got up and closed the curtains and took a sip of her afternoon scotch.

"Ma, you realize you're not talking about a Brit, right? He didn't pillage our towns and take our freedom." She used her father's brogue and shook her fist.

"He might as well be one of the dirty bastards."

"Ma!"

"They aren't like us. I protected you from it when you were young, but now it's gone too far."

"Too far?"

"It was fine as long as you were just living with Maggie, but now it's got to stop."

"You love Mrs. Kovak! I lived in her house as often as in ours."

"You were a child!"

"But you still agreed to it!"

"Claire, we were new to town, and you and Maggie had become friends before we knew."

"Before you knew that they were *also Christians?*"

"They aren't part of the Church. They aren't God's."

"Well, if you wanna get technical, then I should really go for one of God's chosen people and marry Moishe Annenberg."

"God forbid!" A glass slammed down on the other end of the phone.

"Have one conversation with Andy." Claire was standing now, far too upset to sit.

"Calm down, dear."

"But you're being ridiculous!"

"You do not talk to your mother that way, Claire." Suddenly, it was Danny speaking. He must've heard the commotion and come to his wife's aid. Peggy had almost certainly taken the scotch off the table and hid it in her apron.

"Dad, tell her!"

"Tell her what? That you're in love with that Protestant bastard?"

She slammed the phone down. The Ryans had just sworn more than they had in Claire's entire life.

"So." Maggie popped her head out of her room. "How'd it go?"

"Ugh!" Claire threw her hands in the air, grabbed her coat, and stormed out the front door.

The knock on the door was frantic. *Oh, no.*

He opened the door and said, "I take it it didn't go well?"

"Wanna go for a drive?" She looked like she'd been doing that thing she did when she was frustrated where she grabbed fistfuls of her hair and scrunched it 'til her knuckles turned white.

"Yeah."

She turned, not waiting for him to grab his jacket. "How'd you do?"

"Not much better than you apparently."

"Did you know they hated each other?"

"No idea. I guess they had dinner once when we were really little. It was bad."

"You were what, four?"

"Probably."

She was silent. Uncharacteristically so. He stopped. "Claire." She turned toward him with a bit of a huff. He held her hands and looked her square in the eye. "We'll try again."

She smiled, hopeful.

But that was merely the first of an endless stream of similar conversations.

"Why don't you spend more time with Bobby and leave that Ryan girl alone?" Mrs. Kovak asked her son.

"Well, Mother, for one thing, Bobby isn't nearly as pretty as Claire —"

"I'm not joking, Andy."

"And I am a grown man, Ma."

She hung up the phone.

"Bobby seems like a nice boy," Mrs. Ryan said.

"Mother, I'm not in love with Bobby."

"You're not in love with Andy either!"

Claire hung up the phone.

"Andy, what on earth are we supposed to do." Claire sat beside him with her head in her hands. It was the April of her last semester of college.

"We could elope."

She looked up at him. "They'd never speak to us again."

"Would you hate that?"

"Yes!"

There was a knock on the door. Peggy put her scotch under the table and took the scarf off her hair as she scurried to the door. She looked through the peep hole and saw Maria Kovak fidgeting on her front stoop.

"Good morning, Maria." She said politely as she opened the door halfway.

"Peggy." Maria shifted back and forth on her feet. Her forehead was scrunched up and her hair was straining against its pins. "May I come in?"

"Of course. I'll put the kettle on."

They sat stiffly in their chairs at Peggy's kitchen table. It helped to have cups of tea in their hands. At least they knew how to handle those. Peggy looked at Maria. She was a quieter woman than Peggy. Peggy always got the impression that strangers couldn't pull so much as a "no" out of a Hungarian. The Irish didn't even have a word for "no." *We answer in essays no matter who we're talking to.* She didn't know that in her own home Maria was just as fiery as Peggy. Peggy noticed Maria's hand shaking. "Are you alright?"

"It's the kids, Peggy." The words came out like a quiet breeze.

"I know. It was fine with Maggie –"

"But now that it's the two of them –"

"Exactly."

Maria slouched back into her chair a bit, like she'd just seriously exerted herself.

"That might be the first thing we've ever agreed on."

Maria gave a shadow of a smile. "I never disliked you, Peggy."

"Don't tell my husband. He thinks you two are…well, wrong."

"Putting it lightly."

"I guess the kids thought we were the best of friends when they were growing up."

"And there's nothing wrong with that as long so they don't run off and get married because of it." Maria leaned forward.

"So what do we do? I don't think Claire's serious anyway. She's sounded shakier and shakier every time we've talked about it."

"I'm thinking of calling Maggie."

"About what? Converting?"

Maria smirked even as her face was hardening. "Peggy, please."

"I'm sorry, slip of the tongue." Peggy patted her lips. "What if the men sat down and had another crack at a conversation?"

"Because you want to convert us, and we want to convert you. There's no middle ground."

Peggy sat back in her chair. "So you'll call Maggie."

"I'll call Maggie."

"No!" Maggie stamped her foot as she said it. Something about arguments with her mother always made her revert back to being a four-year-old.

"Maggie, darling –"

"No, Mother. I'm not doing that to them."

"Just try talking –"

"What about either of them makes you think they'd listen?"

"Peggy says Claire doesn't really love him."

"Mom, let them be."

Claire sat beside Andy on the way to the burger joint on 2nd. "Andy, we don't have any money."

"I've got a whole dollar bill in my pocket, thank you very much."

"I mean for life not burgers."

"Not yet, but I say let's head straight to Nashville after the wedding." He smiled over at her like she was the first blade of grass in the spring.

"Andy, we're alone."

"Our favorite place to be."

A single tear began to stream down her cheek. It was the first sign of a crack in what had been a very thin veil lately. "Andy, I'm not sure." She was sobbing now.

Andy slowed the car and guided it over to the shoulder. He sat looking down at the steering wheel. "You don't mean that."

"I mean," she said quietly, barely audible through her tears. "I mean I'm not sure about you."

Andy was quiet.

"I don't know what I mean. How am I supposed to know what I mean? My own mother won't speak to me. She's never stopped talking in her life."

"Claire."

"And Maggie's hating this. Your mom called her the other day trying to get her to talk to us."

"Claire. Do you want to marry me?"

She stopped, staring straight ahead. "I'm not sure."

"Well, you better be sure."

"Why? Why can't we just carry on as we have been?"

"You and Maggie are graduating, and then what? Either you move home or you get married."

"Very old-fashioned for a musician."

"Claire, be serious. You want to be a teacher. I want to be a singer. Unless you fancy living in a caravan with twenty other people, neither of us will make it on our own. Can you really see yourself living in a caravan?"

"I just need a little time to –"

"That's something we don't have."

"Oh, why are you always so dramatic? Why does everything have to be some grand adventure? Why can't things just be bad sometimes. Or ordinary." Claire looked at him, and her eyes softened. "Why can't things be ordinary." She brushed her hand across his cheek.

"You said it was exciting."

She pulled her hand away. "Right now, I think it's infuriating."

They were quiet. Andy sighed. "I didn't tell you, but I planned to leave school."

"And go where?"

"Home. Or Tennessee. Or Timbuktu. I don't know."

"Neither of us seems to know much of anything. And all the money my parents spent to make sure I knew everything." She tried for a smile. It came out looking a bit too aggressive for Andy's taste. "I just feel like –"

"What?"

"I feel like…"

"Jesus, Claire, spit it out." She'd never seen fear in his eyes before.

She looked at him with wide round eyes. "I was just going to say…I'm sure about it when I'm defending you to my mom. But I'm not sure that I'm sure about it any other time." Her voice trailed off at the end of the sentence.

Andy reached for the keys to turn the car back on. It rumbled for a second as he stared down the road. He looked over at her then back at the road. "I think I'll take you home now." He pulled onto the road.

She was quiet for a minute. "Andy."

"Either you love me or you don't, Claire. It's that simple."

"You don't understand."

"No, I suppose I don't. Because you see I've never loved anyone else. I've never, not even for one second, doubted how much I loved you." He was shouting now.

She threw her hands in the air. "What do you expect me to say to that. How can you expect me to feel that–"

"Because I do." His expression couldn't be cracked by a chisel.

Claire let him sit for a minute before she said, "This is what I was afraid of."

"What?"

"You loving me too much."

"Wow. Conceited."

"I'm not some perfect angel, Andy." She still looked like one though. Even with her hair frazzled and her mascara just starting to run.

"Lord knows I'm aware of that."

"Are you? Do you know that I went out with Bobby Crawley not one month before you got here?"

"Bobby?"

"Did you know that I've thought about him from time to time since?"

"Claire, I —"

"Did you know that —"

"Claire, stop." He looked in the rearview mirror almost frantically and pulled the car over again. He slammed it in park, and looked her square in the face. "You went out with Bobby Crawley?"

"Yes."

"And neither of you thought it might be nice to tell me?"

"Andy, you and I've been going out for what? Five months?"

"Five months and twenty-six days."

"See? That's what I mean. I can't even remember how many months it's been and here you are counting it up to the second. You idolize me. And I'm not being vain when I say it. It scares me to death." She tried to put her hand on his shoulder. He shrugged it away. "Andy." She tried to catch his eye. He was avoiding her eyes. *How old is he?* "I need more time. I've liked other men before. I need more time to —"

"More time for what? To see if you love Bobby Crawley more than me?"

"To see when the glass will shatter." The feeling had first crept up on her two weeks into dating Andy. It was the way he looked at her. The way he batted away any self-deprecating comments she made. The way he made excuses for everything she did. It felt like he worshipped her. Like, to him, she was perfect. She didn't want to be there when he realized that she wasn't. He wouldn't love her if he didn't think she was perfect.

He looked at her. Examined her. She looked away. She felt like cracks were forming on her face. Slipping through the cracks was her pride. Her whining. Her indecision. She felt him seeing these things for the first time. She felt naked.

"I'll take you home."

"Surely you can't be mad at each other forever." Maggie plopped down in the chair opposite Claire.

"Believe me, I think at least he can."

"But he's your best friend."

"You're my best friend!"

Maggie smirked at Claire. "I'm not, though. I'm co-best friend with my brother."

"It just all happened so quickly. I mean one minute, he's your idiot brother, and the next we're talking about getting married."

Maggie's face flattened. "You hurt him, Claire."

Claire paused. "I know." She fiddled with the hem of her dress. "The weird thing is, I don't think any of this ever would've come up if it weren't for the parents."

"No?"

"No. I think we would've gotten gradually closer, maybe, having little fights and growing to accept each other's faults along the way. I just needed more time."

"Or maybe either way you're my brother's god, and you could never love him as much as he loves you and our parents hate each other and it would've ended anyway. You would've just wasted more time."

Claire looked at the ground.

Maggie got up from the chair. "Well, whatever happens, you've got to perk up. You look utterly ridiculous with that frown on your face."

"It's a simple question, Bobby."

"Yeah, I took her out. Every guy in school at least tried to take her out. But no one got anywhere, if that helps. I just assumed you knew that." Bobby was leaning against the wall of his dormitory room. He was annoyingly self-assured and calm. Andy hated that about him at the moment. But then again, he hated everything about everybody on this particular day.

"Everyone?" Andy was sitting on the bed, trying with all his might to remain still. His leg kept bouncing up and down with nervous energy.

"Christ's sake, man, you're not the only guy she's gone out with."

Andy looked up at his friend. "She's the only one for me."

"Oh, stop. You sound like a shitty romance novel."

Andy got up and started pacing.

Claire graduated with honors. The Ryan family had never been in such a flurry in all their years on earth, what with the feasting and the gifting and the shouting. Relatives from all over the city came out of the woodwork, as random relatives are wont to do, to see the first Ryan ever to graduate from college.

"Ma! Where's the meat?"

"Clairy, honey, we're so proud!" She got smothered with so many kisses, her face was smeared red from the lipstick.

Claire found it odd to be sitting back in the kitchen of her childhood after the changes during four years at school. There were no Ryan children left now who were small enough to hide behind the woodstove. It looked bare to her, like it was missing the shadow of a little red-headed kid.

"And I hear they're looking for an English teacher here at your old high school, Clairy!"

Claire blinked a minute and turned her head away from the stove. "What?"

Claire was hiding from her overzealous relatives while her mother finished up the meal. Her mother's hands were on her hips, which were wider now than they'd been when Claire started university. "I said, Miss Head-in-the-clouds, that Mrs. Morris told me the other day that there's a vacancy at your old school." She shook the spoon in her left hand at Claire. "But you'll not get the job skulking like this."

"I know, Mother." Claire's voice was distant, appearing as if through a thick fog.

Peggy Ryan sighed, waved the spoon in the air, and plopped down beside her daughter. "Claire," she said as she took Claire's hands in her own, spoon still in hand, "He might never write back, Dear."

Claire looked up. Her mother's tone had softened more than it had since before she told her about Andy. Claire's lip began to quiver a bit. *Dammit*, Claire thought as she wiped her hand across her eyes. She must've written to Andy at the Kovak's house thirty times since graduation, and she hadn't heard a word from him.

"Oh, my darling." Peggy took Claire's face in her hands and stared straight into her eyes before wrapping her up in her arms. "I know I didn't want you to marry him. I know you loved him a little. But I know another thing, too – there'll be others."

"Not like him, though."

"Now you listen to me." Peggy held her daughter at arm's length now for effect. "If you were doubting it then, you'd be doubting it all the way down the aisle, and across the threshold, and every day thereafter. Best you broke it off now than to always be wondering if you did the right thing."

"But I'll always be wondering that anyway." Claire wiped her hand across her cheeks.

Her mother brushed her hair out of her eyes and took a handkerchief out of her apron pocket. She dabbed the handkerchief under Claire's eyes as she said, "Ryan women don't sit around wondering. We get up and do." Claire let a shadow of a smile cross her face. "He wasn't the one, dear. Want to know how I know?"

Claire sniffled. "How?"

"Because if he was, he'd be the one here drying your eyes, not me."

Andy poked the ashes of the fire over and over with the poker, jabbing at the bits of wood that had been sitting there since March.

"Andy?"

He didn't look up.

"Andy, do you want to go for a walk?"

He was silent.

"Do you want something to eat?"

Silence.

"Do you –"

"No, dammit! I don't want anything, Maggie." He barely turned his head toward her.

"Alright, you don't have to bite my head off." Her voice drifted away down the hall. Andy stabbed the remnants of the log a few more times. Then he dropped the poker, grabbed his hat, and left.

He arrived in front of the tavern and looked through the window. *No Danny Ryan.* He took of his hat and walked in.

"Top o' the mornin', Laddie!" Mr. O'Flattery stood behind the bar in the same place he'd stood since perhaps the dawn of time. Andy gave him a nod and headed for the piano.

Andy's summer holiday had so far consisted of skulking about his family home. He paced the living room almost constantly, only stopping to move the needle every time the record of Nat King Cole singing "Nature Boy" stopped on the Victrola. He was sitting down to play that very song now. He rolled up his sleeves and rolled into the chords, a haunting melody, brooding. "*We spoke of many things, fools and kings.*" When he'd first heard it on the radio, he'd laughed. He thought Nat King Cole must've been jilted by Claire Ryan, too.

Three months, no letters. *How could she?* He hit the keys of the piano harder.

"Easy there, Laddie." Mr. O'Flattery's voice bellowed over the bar.

Andy buried his face closer to the keys, waltzing into a virtuosic piano break. O'Flattery shook his head and muttered, "If he breaks the damn thing it's comin' outta his paycheck. Poor fellow."

Every day for three months, Andy had asked his mother if she'd had any letters from Claire. "None," she'd answer quietly. He'd stare off into the fire. He'd do that more and more as the years progressed.

"Mother." Claire waltzed through the front door, triumphantly slamming her hat down on the table. "I'm going to teach. Mrs. Morris gave me the job at the high school."

Claire's mother was taking an enormous breath in preparation to launch into a long wave of praise when the telephone rang. "I'll get it!" Claire shouted as she whisked off to the phone. "Hello, Ryan household."

"Hiya, Claire," said a voice that sounded like it was coming from one of those silhouette cutouts of cowboys they have standing coolly in the corners of cheap, mock saloons.

"Bobby?" Claire caught her mother's eye. Peggy made a face of shock. Claire shrugged her shoulders. "How the heck are you?"

"Fine, Claire, just fine. Finer if you can fix a problem for me."

"What's up?"

"Well, you see, I'm in town, and I'm missing school terribly, and I thought maybe we could chat about the good old days."

"The good old days being three months ago?" Peggy batted a hand in Claire's direction that meant *Hush*. "Of course, I'm missing them, too." Claire got a *that's better* face from her mother. "And I'm missing you." She rolled her eyes at her mother's thumbs up and turned her back on her.

"Yeah? I thought we could go to a concert. I know you like music. There's a symphony playing on your side of town."

"Sounds great!"

"Pick you up Saturday at eight? I remember your address."

"I'll look forward to it." Claire hung up the phone and turned to see her mother beaming.

"I asked Mother Mary for a man to come into your life and look! Here he is!" Peggy crossed herself.

"Ma, I've been single for three months, I'm not sure it's exactly a miracle 'til I'm an old maid."

"You hush your mouth, Claire, and go get me your best dress. I'll press it for you."

Bobby sat next to Claire, perilously close to cracking. He wiped his sweaty hands on his trousers and ran his hand through his meticulously gelled hair. If he'd been asked, he would *not* have admitted to having styled it after Andy's hair. Here's the thing about Bobby – Andy thought he was cool. Everyone else just thought he was quiet. Sweet, but quiet. Bobby knew that Claire had gotten her opinion of him from the things Andy said, and he didn't want to break that glass just yet. Yeah, he'd been on a date with her before, but they'd just gone to dinner and a movie that time. He'd made her laugh, asked her about her family, all the standard things. He'd gotten far enough to kiss her goodnight, but that was the end of that. Now, here he was, round two and no new moves. He felt as though he'd performed some kind of magic trick, and his audience was about to figure out how he'd done it.

He strained his eyes to the side to look at her. A vision. Her green dress was dropped off her shoulders a bit, making her shoulders look like they were begging his hand to cover them. He'd never been this nervous in his life. Her hair was all over the place in the most perfect way. Her lips were slightly parted as she watched the symphony in awe. He breathed in sharply as she turned to him and smiled. He turned red as she leaned close to his ear and whispered, "Thank you." He looked at her like she was the night sky, like she was the stars – impossible to see all of her at once, infinitely beautiful, full of magic.

"Oh, that was thrilling!" Claire was saying as she jumped up onto the short stone wall that circled a fountain outside the concert hall.

"Careful, Claire!" Bobby rushed forward, flushed, and grabbed her hand to steady her as she walked around the edge of the fountain in her heels. He was taller than Andy and not as lean. Andy was lean and blond; Bobby was stocky and dark, tanned and a little coarse like he'd spent most of his life outside.

"Come on!" she said as she tried to hoist Bobby up beside her.

"No, no. Can't be getting my best suit wet. But I'll hold your hand while you do it."

Claire balanced her right foot just above the water. Bobby was nice. Very nice. Always quick to help. And not unfine – he had a very gentlemanly manner. She thought she remembered something about… "Weren't you raised on a farm?"

"I was," he said proudly, squeezing her hand tighter as she drifted closer to the edge of the wall.

"Right outside the city, wasn't it?"

"Yep, raised pigs and lugged 'em into market every day. But my mother wanted me to work in the city." He looked proud when he talked about his mother.

"Who will manage the farm when your father retires?" She was fixated on his hair, nice chocolate brown stuff, slicked back in a rather fancy-looking way.

"Oh, my older brother will do that. I always had a head for figuring. Mum wanted me to be an accountant."

Claire fought back the memory of a conversation with Andy about how offices are where men go to die. "Won't it be hard to work in an office after growing up outside?"

Bobby thought for a minute. "Well, I suppose so. But I plan to do plenty of fishing on the weekends."

At this moment Claire's heel caught on the break between stones, and with a cry she was falling toward the water. In a movement that reminded Claire of a rancher scooping up a calf, Bobby pulled on her arm and clutched her to him back from the fountain's edge. "Egad!" said Bobby.

"Oh!" Claire said as she found herself in Bobby's arms. "Fishing?"

"Yes, fishing." Bobby laughed at her abruptness. His face was very close to hers.

"Pity I didn't fall in. You could've practiced." The twinkle in Claire's eye came back.

No letters. Not one goddamn one. "Are you sure?" he asked his mother time and time again.

"Nothing," she'd reply. What Andy couldn't see as he turned his face back toward the empty fire-grate were his mother's paper-filled hands shifting behind her back.

In September of that year, Andy finally had enough. There he'd been, walking along in a slightly-less-angry-than-usual mood, when Bobby and Claire came walking around the corner, arm-in-arm. He stopped dead in his tracks and fixed up his face into a glare to rival Medusa, but she didn't see him. She was smiling at Bobby. Andy stared at the backs of their heads hard enough to bore a hole into them then turned on his heel and raced back home.

A great commotion could be heard as he dragged out his suitcase and slammed it on the bed. He grabbed all the clothes in his closet and yanked them messily off their hangers in one sweep. "What in God's name?" he could hear Maggie shout as she came running up the stairs.

She stopped breathless in his doorway. "What the hell are you doing?"

"Maggie! Language!" their mother shouted from downstairs.

"Mom, Andy's running away from home," Maggie called over her shoulder.

Andy hurled a tie her way, which fluttered to the ground many feet in front of her nose.

"I asked, where are you going?"

"Away."

"Ah, thought this through well, I see."

"Piss off."

"Be nice."

Andy stopped, his arms full of music sheets he'd just scooped up off of his desk. "I'm sorry, Maggie." He didn't look at her. "I can't stay here. I'll die."

"Die?" Just then, their mother appeared at the top of the staircase. "Should I get the castor oil?"

"No! I'm not sick," he went to throw his hands in the air, remembered the music, and put it in the suitcase instead.

"Then stop being so dramatic," Maggie said.

"I'm going to New York."

"New York!" His mother was wringing her hands. To Mrs. Kovak, New York symbolized every evil in the world. It was the melting pot of every sin.

"I've got to." And so he did.

"Look at this!" Bobby lowered the corner of his newspaper to look at Claire.

She nearly dropped her tea as she asked, "Who died?"

"No, no. Andy Kovak, front page." He turned the paper around and flashed it open for her. There he was. A tortured looking soul in black and white pounding away at a piano, his head thrown back, mouth open as he sang. The headline read "Chicago Boy Conquers New York Nightclub Scene." They were sitting in the Ryans kitchen at the breakfast table. He'd come to have breakfast with the family, but they'd left a while ago to give the lovebirds time alone together.

"Boy howdy," Bobby whistled. "'Andy Kovak, a college drop out from the immigrant quarter, brings to New York a new taste for jazz. His vocal prowess coupled with his gift for tinkling the ivories is turning some of the biggest heads in the city. 'Andy has a way of sighing out his songs one minute and screaming them from the bottom of his soul the next,' says talent agent.'" Bobby whistled again. "I'm glad to hear the old boy's doing well for himself."

Claire was stirring her tea.

"It's so odd seeing someone you know in the news. I mean I know it's only such a big deal 'cause a Chicago boy's making it big. But egad!"

"Mmm." Claire was looking down.

Bobby started reading another line from the story. *It's been two years.* It shouldn't be a big deal anymore. But Claire felt her heart start pounding when she looked at the picture.

"I miss that guy. I know things ended bad, but, boy, we had fun." Bobby looked up, puzzled by Claire's uncharacteristic silence. His face suddenly grew very soft. "I'm sorry. I wasn't thinking." He reached a hand across the table to her. "What are *you* thinking."

"Oh, it's nothing," she squeezed his hand. "Just a lot of un-answered letters."

"But it's ok now?"

"It's wonderful now." She shot her Irish eyes at him with a smile.

"Andy there's something I have to tell you." Andy thought he heard his sister's voice quaver. He held the receiver away from his mouth and sighed. *This is gonna be about her.*

"What?" he asked, trying to sound casual but sounding impatient instead.

He heard her take a big breath on the other end of the line. *Oh boy,* he thought right before he heard Maggie say, "Claire's getting married."

He sat quietly, his head rested on his hand.

"Andy?"

"Yeah, I'm here." He felt an edge creeping into his voice.

"Yeah, but are you ok?"

"I have to be, don't I?"

"Dramatic as always." He could hear her smile in her voice, but the comment frustrated him anyway.

"Am I allowed one minute of frustration without being called a crying pansy?"

"Sorry! Geez, Andy. I didn't mean to upset you."

"It's fine." He found himself feeling more and more numb. "I gotta go. I've got a show tonight."

"Alright, love you."

"Hm," he huffed as he put down the phone.

He stood up and walked to the fridge in his kitchen. If Maggie had been there to see it, she would've screamed. The floor was almost completely covered with paper bags, beer bottles, and newspapers. He looked like a canary living in a birdcage. And he sang like one, too. Every night he left his shit-hole apartment in a suit that cost a month's rent. He walked himself downtown, being careful to step around every puddle for fear of it not being water, and lit a cigarette as he swung in through the stage door of whatever club he was singing at that night.

Now, in preparation, he flicked open the first beer of his typical three drink minimum before going on to sing. He started at about two o'clock so he would be all liquored up by the time the audience saw him. *I think a few more tonight,* he thought as he threw back the first, then the second, then the third.

He didn't talk to people as a general rule. He didn't have to try very hard to avoid that, working nights. He didn't know what his neighbors looked like let alone what their names were.

A few hours later he was washed, shaved, coiffed, and liquored, walking his way downtown. He ran up the stairs tonight to the back door and nodded to the manager. His "ruffled" look, as the papers called it, added to his appeal with the female audience, so no one minded his drinking and smoking as long as he showed up on time.

He did his shtick. He moaned about lost love, laughed about lost friends, and shouted at lost opportunity, and by the time the night was over, there were four women begging to buy him a drink.

"C'mon, Andy, let me buy you a beer," giggled one of them.

"No thanks, honey. I'm going home." He waved to the manager and swung his jacket over his arm.

He kept this up 'til the beer settled in his gut, and he suddenly found he didn't fit as cleanly into his suits as he used to. When that happened, he went to recording his songs so no one would have to look at the fat, balding man he'd become. He hated his life, but he made a million. And he talked to fewer and fewer people with every drink he drank.

And so, here we are back where we started. Claire stared into the casket and lived her entire life as she looked at Andy's face. She'd heard in a newspaper years ago that he'd become an alcoholic, and to be honest, he looked it. *I should've asked someone.* But it was too late. She was already on her way home. She'd thought about staying the night, but she felt like she needed to be at home. She leaned her head back against the seat of the train. She thought about Maggie. She hadn't seen her there. *Must've missed her.* Once every few months for years and years and years, she and Maggie met up for lunch. The Kovaks had done well for themselves, particularly Maggie and Andy. Only people who do have that kind of greedy, uncouth relative come out of the woodwork when one of them dies. There was an understandable and unspoken agreement between Maggie and Claire that there was to be no Andy-talk. The feeling of awkwardness that arose whenever they stumbled upon topics like music, religion, relationships, family, the evening, blond people, and the city of New York had vanished years ago. But Claire had no idea that Andy had been ill. She had no idea that he had become a friendless and sad old man, other than her own personal inklings that he wasn't doing well. If she was very honest with herself, she thought drink sounded like something his passionate soul would find solace in. Her face was covered in a rain cloud. Passersby would've thought "Eeyore" if they'd looked at her. But there were no passersby to think anything about her or the state of her face on this late train out of the city.

She walked into her kitchen quietly. It was more early morning than late evening, and she didn't want to disturb Bobby.

"I would've liked to go, too, you know."

Claire jumped and put her hand to her heart, "Christ, you scared me." Bobby was sitting at the kitchen table. The coffee pot was still on in the corner.

"Sorry," he said as he got up from his seat. "I didn't mean to frighten you. He was my friend once, too, you know."

Claire noticed the newspaper in his hand. "I'm sorry." She put her bags down by the door.

"Maggie hadn't said anything?"

"No. It was a long time ago, Bobby." She walked over to him and leaned her head against his shoulder. "I am sorry, though. I just needed…"

"I understand." He always understood. She kissed his shoulder and pressed her face tighter against his jacket.

"Claire?"

A tear was dampening his jacket. She didn't answer.

"Have you been happy?"

Claire looked up at him. She put all her resolve in her eyes, which is saying something. "I'll not deny it. I loved him, Bobby. I loved his passion, his fervor, his life."

"All things I'm short on."

"Bobby." She put her hand on his cheek. "How long have we been married?"

"Fifty years," they said in unison. She went on, "Of course I've been happy, you great oaf. He may have had a couple traits in abundance, but you have everything."

They stood in their kitchen, a little worse for the wear. It had been hard. Claire's zest often overpowered Bobby. She wore the pants, as they say. But it worked for them, and they were very rarely unhappy. In fact, as they held each other and stared each into the other's eyes, they were some of the happiest.

"I'm going to call Maggie in the morning," Claire said as Bobby stroked her smooth, gray hair.

"Wasn't she there?"

"I'm sure she was, but I missed her. Nothing but money-grabbers by the time I got there."

"I guess he left quite the fortune."

"Yes! If I'd married him, I could've had a mink coat, a mink sofa, mink sheets." Her eyes twinkled.

Bobby reached down and held her face in his hands, "You Irish nut."

In the corner of the usual restaurant, drinking the usual tea, with the usual waitress taking their usual order, sat two kind-looking old women. They had a broken familiarity about them – a new awkwardness to an old, old friendship.

"Why didn't you tell me?" Claire asked Maggie.

"I was afraid. It's been fifty years since we've talked about any of it." Maggie had just finished painting a picture of a crotchety old man sitting on his porch, shaking his fist at the children running across his freshly cut grass. She talked about a man who'd been a playboy for a time until his destructive qualities drove even the greediest women away. She talked about a man who could sing, but only because he was shattered inside.

"What I still don't understand is why he never wrote back," Claire said as she sipped some more tea. Her voice had gotten grayer, too – a little more coarse but still full of life.

Maggie hesitated. "I know." She started fidgeting with her napkin.

"You know?" Claire put down her cup and leaned forward.

"Not until, oh, I guess it was fifteen years ago now. She lived for forever, God bless her."

"Who?"

"Mom. I found your letters in a box when Mom died."

There was silence. Claire stared straight past Maggie.

"Would it have changed anything?" Maggie asked. "You and Bobby had been married for thirty-some years by then."

"Almost forty."

"Forty years. You don't stay with someone for forty years just because you were kept from someone else."

"You think I regret something?"

"You look like you do."

"Maggie," Claire reached her hands toward her friend. "Look at my hands." They were wrinkled, and the veins stuck up high from the bones. "I'm much too old for regrets."

Maggie held Claire's hands with her own wrinkled pair and asked, "But did you ever?"

A Picture

There's a woman that lives with her husband down the street. They've been married and living there for longer than anyone can remember. All those who would know left long ago. There's a very faded sign by the front door that says "The Crawleys, est. 19—," and if you squint very hard you might be able to figure out the year. Every morning, the husband brings a cup of coffee and a tray table with scrambled eggs and a flower from the front garden in a tall cup to his wife as she sits in bed. The wife smiles and takes the comics section of the paper that he hands to her. He then goes back to the kitchen to read the rest of the paper. The woman is full of fire, a little slower burning these days, but it's never totally gone out. The man has a smile for everyone he meets. But no one brings the brightness into his eyes that his wife does.

Neighbors like to make up stories about their past. The couple doesn't say much about their younger years. They prefer to live in the moment, for it is so short. Everyone thinks the woman will work until the day she dies, and the husband is content to be retired now, doing the cooking and cleaning that his wife never cared for. I once asked them about regret. The woman told me there's simply no time for it. "Regret haunts you. And who wants ghosts hanging around?" Her husband smiled from his place at the kitchen table and reached out to hold his wife's hand.

About the Author

Juliana Nicewarner is the daughter of a Marine, which means that she has lived in twenty-odd houses in her twenty-odd years. She has pursued many things in her life, working as everything from a logistics manager for guiding companies to an equine veterinary assistant. She has to stay busy, and while the one constant passion in her life has been writing, she continues to pursue anything and everything she can. She lives in Denver where she is the singer and manager of a Colorado-based jazz band, works as a substitute teacher, is a sometimes editor, and an all the time writer. Her work has been published in local travel guides and more than once by Adelaide Literary Magazine. Her passion is for reading and writing well-written stories that focus on the real and the inexplicable things encountered in everyday life.